BLACK PAD

Nicola Payne pulled apart the curtains of her home on Winston Avenue and shivered. She could barely make out the houses on the other side of the road through the heavy early morning mist. A neighbour was out walking his dog just as he did every day. Both were wrapped in coats ... one with sleeves for two arms and the other with gaps for four legs. The coats might help keep them warm but there was nothing to be done to penetrate the increasingly dense haze outdoors.

Nicola was not particularly concerned about the cold, murky conditions. Her parents had helped her choose a winter coat from the newly opened Debenham's store in West Orchards and it was a snug, comfortable fit.

Her seven-month-old son, whom she and her partner had named Owen, was fast asleep. Nicola had barely turned eighteen when she gave birth and, to the undisguised delight of her parents, had embraced her new role as a young mother and partner to Jason with unprecedented ease.

Nicola glanced at her watch. Yet another present from her doting parents. Nine thirty. Once she'd finished drinking her cup of tea, she'd be off.

She called out to Jason, "I'm going shortly. Don't forget Owen's mid-morning mashed banana."

"Send them both my love," Jason responded.

*

2

He and Nicola had met each other whilst attending the same school and had soon formed a close and intimate friendship that had resulted in a pregnancy eleven months earlier. Jason was a good lad and an attentive father, and Nicola's parents took to him having seen how much he cared for their daughter and adored his baby son.

Nicola opened the front door and was greeted by Coventry's foggy winter morning. It would probably clear by the afternoon for her return journey. She shivered, not only from the cold nip in the air, but from the thought of crossing the area known to locals as *The Black Pad*.

The Black Pad is said to have got its name because it the path running through it was used to take coal to Carlton Hayes Hospital. It begins at All Saints Church, travels in an almost straight line past the cemetery, across the King Edward Avenue bypass to the junction with Forest Road and on to the start of a footpath called *'Ten Pound Lane'* in the direction of Enderby.

"Make sure you keep an eye on Owen, won't you?" she called back over her shoulder.

"And you make sure to keep an eye out for cyclists and bad car drivers in all that fog," Jason replied. "There are some crazy people on the roads round here."

He heard the door bang shut and turned to the pram in the narrow hallway.

"It's just you and me this morning, kiddo," he told the sleeping child. "Lucky for you that I work nights." He would take a nap himself mid-morning after Nicola had returned.

The date was Thursday, 14th of December 1991.

※

Nicola's parents were named Marilyn and John and she knew how fortunate she was that they lived no more than a brisk ten-minute walk away from the small house that they had purchased for her and Jason.

Jason was a little older than Nicola and worked most evenings at a local supermarket stacking shelves ready for the following day's shoppers, leaving Nicola to bathe and put Owen in his cot most nights. On his days off, Jason enjoyed carrying out these routines himself.

Nicola pulled her coat tighter and began the short walk through the mist towards the track that ran across the wasteland known locally as the *Black Pad*. The only reason for this morning's trip was that her mother had purchased some new clothes for Owen and she looked forward to collecting them. She could not have known that cold, impassive eyes had been watching her house, day after day, waiting for just such a moment as this.

The Christmas season was fast approaching, and Nicola felt her excitement growing as she eagerly anticipated her first Christmas with Jason, Owen and her own family.

It was unusually quiet for a Saturday on the *Black Pad*. There were normally a few dogs being taken for a walk, or kids kicking a ball around, but the foggy conditions seemed to have acted as a deterrent on this particularly chilly December morning.

Nicola figured she was almost halfway along an uneven track when she tripped on a short length of rope that was stretched between two wooden tent pegs.

The rope was shrouded by the low-lying fog and she was sent crashing into the rough grass and weeds that lined her route.

※

Nicola's mother kept glancing out of the front room window of her home in Woodway Close. She had been expecting Nicola's arrival for the past thirty minutes and her daughter hadn't phoned to say she might be late. The phone sat silently on a shelf in the hallway.

She called out to her husband.

"Can you hear me, dear? Just check that the phone's working, would you?"

She heard the living room door open on its squeaky hinges followed by her husband's footsteps in the hall.

A few moments later he replied, "the phone's working fine. Why do you ask?"

"It's Nicola. I expected her to have arrived by now."

"Have you forgotten already what it's like to have a demanding baby to fuss over? You know how she dotes over him"

"She has Jason!" his wife retorted.

His wife, Marilyn then grinned mischievously. "But, of course, he's a man. What do men know about bringing up babies?"

The minutes and then the hours crept by.

※

Jason had had a phone line installed in the simple two-bedroomed home he and Nicola were purchasing following an exceptionally generous contribution from her parents. House prices in Coventry had dropped dramatically in 1990 and Nicola's parents pointed out that their purchase was an investment opportunity as well as providing the young family with a home.

*

Jason had put aside a portion of his weekly income until he had sufficient to have a phone line installed. He wasn't expecting Nicola to phone him as she was likely to return within the next hour or two so he was surprised to hear its shrill ring from the living room. He walked briskly from the kitchen hoping the sudden jangle of the phone hadn't awakened Owen.

"Hello. It's Jason."

"Jason ... it's Nicola's mother. Is Nicola with you?"

"Well, no. Nicola should be with you." He glanced at his wristwatch. "She left here more than an hour ago."

"Well, she hasn't arrived, and John says not to worry. He thinks she might have stopped off to do a spot of shopping."

"Nicola never mentioned it," Jason replied.

"Do you think she might have lost her way in the fog?"

"I would hardly think so. She could find her way to your house with her eyes closed."

"But in this fog ...?"

"In this fog it would probably be a lot safer for her to keep her eyes *open*, Mrs Payne."

"Yes, of course. Did she say which route she was taking to get here?"

"Well, I assumed it would be the route she always takes ... over the *Black Pad*."

"I keep telling her it isn't safe in the dark and this fog is just as bad. She might have tripped and fallen. She might have hurt herself. She might ..."

"Okay, dear, that'll do," John Payne said. "I could hear you from next door. If it'll make you happy, I'll go see if I can find her. How about that?"

"Would you? I'd really appreciate that. It's just not like Nicola. She's usually so picky about people being punctual."

"I'd go myself," Jason said, "but the ground's too uneven for the pushchair you kindly bought for Owen."

"Don't worry. John's just said he's going to look for her."

11

She heard the front door open and close.

"He's just left. I'll call you as soon as they're both back."

John Payne had no inkling that his home was being watched.

※

Almost an hour had passed and Mrs Payne's anxiety was mounting rapidly.

Eventually, it became too much for her, so she phoned Jason.

"Is John with you?"

"No, he isn't. You told me he was going out to find where Nicola had got to."

"Well, he hasn't returned!"

The line fell silent ... the silence finally broken by Jason.

"Okay. I'll put Owen in his pushchair and take a look. I don't expect to actually see much in this fog and it'll be a bumpy ride for Owen. Anyway, I'll leave now and take the route Nicola usually takes across the *Black Pad*. Stay home, though, because I'll drop by with her once I've found her. I hope to be with you in about twenty minutes assuming Owen behaves himself."

"With Nicola?"

"I damn well hope so!"

Owen began to yowl almost as soon as Jason picked him up. For once, Jason lost patience with his young son.

"Christ! Do be quiet!" Jason said irritably as he tried strapping Owen into the pushchair. He forgot to apply the handbrake and it trundled forward sending him sprawling onto the wooden floor. His chin hit the hard surface and he cried out in pain. He struggled to his feet, dazed and angry.

At the rate he was going he would never make it to work on time let alone find two missing souls and manage a bawling kid.

※

Jason rang Nigel Barwell. Nigel was another of the night crew and they enjoyed an uneasy relationship.

Occasionally, they might go for a drink together before starting their night shift at the supermarket. There was something devious about Nigel and Jason didn't go out of his way to encourage their friendship.

"It's me, mate. Jason. Nicola set out to pick up some clothes my mother-in-law has bought for Owen. Her mother has just phoned to say she hasn't turned up and her husband's gone out looking for her. I'm in a bit of a mess here. I've taken a tumble and cut my chin. Once I've sorted myself out, I'll take Owen out and see if I can find Nicola. I know you sometimes take a route to work across the *Black Pad*. If you do, would you keep a lookout for her?"

"No worries, mate. Anything to help out a friend."

※

Nicola was dazed and angry, too.

15

She had tripped on something that lay hidden from sight across the track. The fog was thicker than any she could recall. She struggled to her feet and rubbed her chin. It might be grazed. It certainly stung and felt sore when she touched it.

There was blood on her hand.

She raised her wristwatch to eye-level, glanced at the time and frowned.

Her parent's house was now no further than a painful five- or six-minutes' walk away. They were sure to have something to rub onto her chin. They had a bathroom cabinet stuffed full of potions, lotions, plasters and pills.

Nicola heard a *whooshing* sound from close by and an instant later was knocked unconscious by the impact of a heavy hammer that fractured her skull and left her torso twitching until finally laying still.

※ ※※

Marilyn Payne knew she was panicking. It was the same feeling she had experienced after mislaying her wedding ring the previous year. She knew she had put on quite a bit of weight, what with her penchant for chocolate and cream-filled cakes, and her fingers had thickened. The ring was tight and often left her finger swollen. It needed taking to the jeweller in town to be resized.

She and John had spent the best part of a frustrating thirty minutes coaxing the ring from her finger and then he'd gone out to get his Wednesday *Daily Mail* for its puzzle page. She'd put the ring down on the armrest of the sofa in their front room whilst she went upstairs to the medicine cabinet to fetch some liniment to rub into her sore finger. When she returned ... the ring was not there! John would be *really* cross with her for being so careless. She had tried squeezing her hand down the side of the sofa ... felt no ring ... and then struggled to pull her hand back up. That was when the panic rose within her. John would say she should have left it for him to deal with. He was good at dealing with problems. She continued to search frantically for the ring. Her heart was pounding, her hands trembled, her head felt as if it was buzzing ... she'd never, ever felt such a loss of control.

It had taken her an hour of frenetic searching before remembering that she had put it in her purse, in her handbag, ready to take to town next day.

And now that feeling of panic was replicating itself. Nicola had not arrived to collect Owen's baby clothes; Jason hadn't knocked on the front door with Owen in his pushchair and she didn't know whether her husband had come across any of them. Her emotions ran high and were beginning to gallop out of control.

※

John Payne strained his eyes to pierce the thick fog but to no avail. He'd feel silly calling out Nicola's name into this bleak nothingness, assuming his voice would penetrate the misty blanket sufficiently to be heard. He was in two minds whether or not to continue his stumbling search over the *Black Pad* or return to the welcoming warmth back home. Of course, he'd have to face Marilyn's questions and she would be angry that he could only provide negative answers.

Which is when *he* tripped and fell heavily on to the damp track. Cursing, he began to scramble back on to his knees. Thank goodness the ground was soft. Soft but far from dry. He turned his head to see what had caused him to take a tumble ... which is when he spotted a short length of rope secured between two wooden stumps across the worn pathway. He recognised them as tent pegs. Who the hell had put that there? And why? It had to be intentional. Could you imagine? Somebody had thought it funny to go out into the dense fog and deliberately stretch a rope across the track. And whoever it was hadn't even stayed to laugh at the result of his handiwork. Or maybe he had. Maybe he was out there, concealed by the mist and laughing to himself. Or herself.

With creaking knees, he began to rise from the rough grass, now very wet and dressed in water vapour. He never made it back onto his feet because something thudded against the back of his head and he crashed, senseless, back onto the damp ground.

※ ※ ※

Nigel Barwell was pleased with his morning's work.

The dense fog had proved an unexpected bonus. He opened both the rear doors of his rusty old van and dragged Nicola's body off the flat, four-wheeled wooden trolley he'd nicked from the supermarket where both he and Jason worked. After pausing for breath, he frowned. How was he to get her over the van's tailgate? He cursed himself for not thinking things through. He needed an improvised ramp. He didn't have one. He wasn't even certain she was dead. The hammer blow had smashed her skull and blood had spurted across her face and shoulders but he hadn't thought to check her breathing. Suppose she regained consciousness and began screaming? Not that it mattered a great deal in his grand scheme of revenge.

Another hammer blow should silence her.

Jason had it coming to him. He had it all. A beautiful wife, a baby son, a home that had become his own through the generosity of his in-laws.

What do I have, he asked himself? A van that was falling apart. No female friends. A scruffy flat that cost him half his income.

Nigel grabbed Nicola's ankles, using his strength to drag her the remaining six feet to the rear double-doors of his van. He was more accustomed to dragging trolleys loaded with cans of Coke or tinned food. He opened the passenger door, clambered up into his van, scrambled between its front seats and stumbled towards the double doors at the rear. Damn! They needed to be unlocked ... *but from the outside!* He should have prepared a mental checklist ... but he hadn't ... so he crawled back to the front and out again through the offside door and around to the back of the van ... and unlocked and opened its double doors.

He tugged and lifted Nicola's legs up on to the tailgate. Both the van and his activity were shielded from sight by a power substation at a far corner of the *Black Pad* and, of course, the fog which was still thick even though it was around ten-thirty in the morning.

Nigel was strong and Nicola was slim and short.

Within a few minutes he had hauled her by her legs up onto the floor of the van and dragged her body along towards the front of his van. *I'm evil,* he thought to himself, *but I'm good at it!* He then yanked the trolley up into the van.

Now to deal with Owen's father-in-law. He started the vehicle's engine and headed off.

He'd been watching his house for several days but hadn't detected a pattern. *But then he had got lucky!* Following Jason's phone call to him, he now knew that Nicola's father was heading for *The Black Patch* in search of Nicola. He could kill two birds with one stone. Or one hammer, in this case.

He drove to the man's house, taking care to park out of sight. He watched him cross the road and walk towards the *Black Pad. All looking good!*

He drove back the way he had just come and parked his van, as before, behind the power station.

※

John Payne strained his eyes to pierce the thick fog but to no avail. He'd feel silly calling out Nicola's name into this nothingness, even assuming his voice could penetrate the thick, misty blanket. He was in two minds whether or not to continue his tentative search over the *Black Pad* or to return to the welcoming warmth at his home. Of course, he'd have to face Marilyn's questions and she would be particularly scathing if she learnt he'd abandoned the search. She wanted an answer, not an apology.

… which is when he tripped and fell heavily on to the damp track. Cursing, he tried to raise himself on to his

knees. Thank goodness the ground was soft. Soft but far from dry. He turned his head to see what had caused him to fall ... which is when he spotted a short length of rope secured between two wooden stumps across the well-worn pathway. He recognised them to be tent pegs. Who the hell had put them there? *And why?* It had to be intentional. Someone had thought it amusing to go out into the dense fog and deliberately stretch a piece of rope across the track. And whoever it was hadn't even bothered to hang around long enough to laugh at the end result of their handiwork.

Or maybe they had! Maybe somebody was out there, concealed by the mist, laughing to themselves.

With creaking knees, he began to rise from the rough grass, now very wet and dressed in water vapour. He never made it back onto his feet because something struck the back of his head and he crashed, senseless, back onto the damp ground.

※

Jason pulled the cart out of his van and dragged it back along the path, peering through the near-impenetrable fog, seeking John Payne. He cursed as he almost tripped *himself* up on his own piece of rope!

He spotted his second victim on the ground curled into a letter *'C'*.

Nigel dragged his cart alongside the inert body, raised the man's legs onto it, then jumped aboard and, using every ounce of his strength, pulled John's bulky figure along the surface of the cart. He was now faced with the backbreaking task of pulling his improvised carrier back to the van. The man was a great deal heavier than Nicola Payne.

It was starting to grow dark as he completed the second journey.

He opened the boot's lid and then pulled the man's body by his legs from the cart to the back of his van. John Pain was no lightweight and it took a great deal of effort to yank him up on to the interior floor. *Job done!*

Nigel scrambled to his feet, ducked his head, shuffled forward and squeezed between the front seats. He seated himself behind the steering wheel, started the engine and drove away. *He was a star!*

※

Marilyn Payne was frantic with worry. Where was her

daughter? Where was her husband? Being a mother, a wife and a grandparent was so taxing and the new baby clothes she had been out and bought especially for baby Owen still sat on the sideboard ... and she had given up her time and spent her money choosing them. John never paid for things like that.

It seemed pointless to go out searching for them. If one, or both, should return they would wonder where *she* was and might go out searching for *her*!

※

The fog was slowly lifting as Nigel drove towards his lock-up garage. He was fortunate. The early darkness of a mid-day, mid-December afternoon, cloaked him from inquisitive eyes.

There were six garages set apart for residents of the

three-storey block of flats. Nigel's was at the far end, furthest away from the communal entrance to the aging flats. He reversed on to the shingle that littered the fronts of the lockups, clambered out of his van, unlocked the lift-up door to garage *'1'* and then opened the back doors of his van.

First, he hauled John Payne's body from the vehicle to the rear of the garage and then returned for that of Nicola. He dragged her over the concrete floor and dumped her beside John Payne. He then pulled down the up-and-over garage door and relocked it.

So far, so good, he thought. Everything was working according to his hastily prepared plan. *But he wasn't quite done.*

Nigel drove his van close to Jason's home and parked in a side street. He caught his breath as a police car suddenly sped past with its blue lights flashing but it didn't stop.

He caught his breath a second time as the front door to Jason's home opened and Jason hurried out, turned, and pulled a pushchair over the doorstep. He watched him go back indoors and return a few moments later with a bawling baby in his arms. *Ah, yes, Jason had mentioned a baby to him.* A boy. He must be about six months' old by now. He watched Jason strap the child into the seat of the pushchair and then followed him on foot. Nigel kept his distance, took care not to be seen, and was thankful that the darkening afternoon was closing around him like a black cloak.

※ ※ ※

Nigel couldn't believe his luck. *I acted so quickly*, he

thought to himself. *I acted so swiftly that I wish there was someone I could boast about it to.* Maybe there *is* someone, he mused, as he watched Jason propelling the pushchair along the pavement ... and then he grinned to himself. *He's heading for* the *Black Pad. In the dark!* Perhaps I should warn him of the dangers that might lay lurking in wait. *Perhaps not*!

※

The wailing began almost from the moment Jason put Owen in his pushchair. He loved his baby son, of course he did, but the insistent howling would surely get on *anyone's* nerves. It didn't make him a bad father. As if he wasn't anxious enough already. Nicola's mother had taken to ringing him every ten minutes but matters had got completely out of hand when she added her husband to the list of absentees.

Where the hell were they? Had they both fallen into a deep hole? Were there wild beasts on the prowl, lurking in the darkness looking for their next meal? This was Coventry, for heaven's sake! He'd read that the name *'The Black Pad'* had meant 'dark path' back in the day. It was certainly living up to its name on this cold, darkening afternoon in December.

Owen's crying had drifted into a soft whimper. He was probably hungry and Jason had forgotten to bring his formula milk. Oh, well, it was too late to turn around. After a few minutes, Owen fell asleep and Jason released a huge sigh of relief.

He reached the *Black Pad* and removed a torch from his coat pocket. It emitted a faint beam. The batteries needed replacing. He had stolen a pack from the supermarket where he worked his five-nights-a-week shelf-filling shift but had forgotten to install them. He ought to feel guilty about their theft but he often pilfered and brought home small, inexpensive items that he could slip easily into his pocket. A bar of chocolate, a bag of sweets, a packet of aspirins. He wasn't paid a great deal and felt his actions were justified. He had caught Nigel, his fellow shelf-filler, stealing from the supermarket but to a more serious extent ... a transistor radio, a hairdryer, even an electric shaver. Nigel had threatened to stick a knife in him if he told anyone. Jason kept his distance and kept his mouth shut. Nigel was best avoided.

The journey with a pushchair on an uneven track, still damp from the fog that had clung to the grass and soil, was a bumpy one and Owen began to whimper almost as soon as Jason set off. What was he hoping to find? Nicola? John Payne? Both enjoying a private tea-party sitting on a blanket in the bleak conditions, perhaps?

Having a good time while he slogged along with a pushchair.

Ahead of him lay no more than a ten-minute walk … assuming none of the wheels fell off the pushchair or Owen was whisked away by pixies.

※ ※ ※

John Payne wiped a hand across the back of his head and screwed up his eyes in agony. The pain was intense. The throbbing insistent. His hand was covered in blood and … *he was in darkness*. Not the darkness that night brought because the darkness of a damp, confined space. A damp, confined space that reeked of petrol fumes and … something else. His eyes slowly adjusted to the gloom and his heart skipped a beat. No more than a couple of feet from him lay a body.

"*Nicola!*" he cried out. But the body of his dead daughter had no way of replying.

He staggered up on to his feet. He needed to call an ambulance. He acknowledged it was too late to save his daughter but perhaps it was not too late to save *himself* ... but it meant getting out of what he now recognised was an empty garage ... empty apart from a pile of tools in one corner and a stack of unopened cans of soup, beans, peaches and pears in the other ... and somewhere in between ... his daughter.

He rattled the garage door. It had been locked. He couldn't escape. He needed to call an ambulance. He began shouting.

"*Help! Let me out! Can anyone hear me?*"

❋ ❋ ❋

Jason exited the *Black Pad* and crossed the road, heading for his in-law's house, a hundred yards from where he now stood, with Owen in the pushchair having finally fallen asleep. He looked up. Marilyn Payne, Nicola's mother, was standing on the pavement outside her home. As soon as she spotted Owen approaching, she walked towards him, anxiety unmistakable on her face.

"Did you not find them?" she asked plaintively.

Jason shook his head.

"We have to call the police," Marilyn said. "Something terrible has happened to them. I just know it has."

"We don't know that. It's likely to be a coincidence, nothing more," Jason responded. "Let's give it a little longer."

※ ※ ※

John Payne hammered on the inside of the garage door. Surely somebody would hear him. Somebody from one of the adjoining garages or one of the flats … and then he heard the sound of tyres on gravel close by, a car door opening, a garage lid being raised on its creaking, unoiled hinges.

"Hello! Can you hear me?" he shouted. There was no response, so he tried again. *"Anybody! Can you hear me?"* He hammered on the garage door with clenched fists.

"Are you all right?"

A woman's voice. He wanted to cry out … *"of course I'm not all right! I'm trapped in this garage with my dead daughter!"*

Instead, he asked a dumb question.

"Can you get me out of here? I've been locked in."

He sounded like a young lad being punished for some misdemeanour.

"Oh, dear. I really don't know. I'll ask my husband. Stay where you are."

Stay where I am? As though I had a choice! As if!

He wasn't thinking straight. He should have asked her to call the police, of course, and an ambulance. He needed both services.

John waited impatiently. After what felt to him like an eternity, he heard footsteps approaching on the gravel and a man's voice shouted …

"We'll have you out of there in a jiffy."

A *jiffy* lasted almost thirty minutes and then the up-and-over garage door was raised.

"Thank you," John said. "I need to report a murder."

"Sorry, sir. I'm only a locksmith. I don't deal with murders. You'll need to call the police." The man hesitated and then asked, "you've murdered someone?"

John ignored the man and staggered away. His head was still pounding but the blood on his face had coagulated. He scanned his surroundings and recognised this particular area of Coventry. He'd lived in the city all his life and knew it well. His home was little more than a mile away and he began to walk unsteady towards it.

※

Nigel watched the action from the dark entrance to the pathway that eventually led to the *Black Pad.* Even from a distance of a hundred yards he could hear John Payne shouting and pounding his fists on the inside of the garage door. Nigel was anxious to move Nicola's body from out of the garage. He'd been reading about advances in DNA and he might have left his fingerprints on her clothing. He hadn't thought about that. Another slip-up on his part. *Maybe he wasn't quite as smart as he thought.*

He couldn't believe his luck when a Transit van pulled up by the garages and a man in overalls carrying a bag of tools got out and walked over to the garage where John Payne was trapped. He watched the man fiddle with the door's mechanism. He saw the garage lid rise. He caught sight of John Payne stumbling out and, a few moments later, staggering off in the direction of his home. Nigel knew he had to act quickly. John Payne shouldn't be walking away. *John Payne should be dead! Along with his daughter!*

※

Nigel waited until John Payne was out of sight before driving cautiously towards his garage. As he approached it, he shut off the engine and cruised to a halt on the gravel, one garage along, allowing him room to move Nicola's body straight from the garage and through the open back doors of his van. He knew he would need to act quickly. It might be no more than a minute or two before a police car rounded the corner, blue lights flashing. No doubt, it would be closely shadowed by an ambulance.

The garage had been left unsecured. Nigel assumed the

locksmith would return to replace the mechanism tomorrow maybe ... *but not in the next five minutes.* He would probably return in the morning when he could work without a torch.

Nigel couldn't have made it across to his garage unseen had it not been December. Few locals wanted to venture out unnecessarily on a cold, winter's evening and those that did made use of their cars.

He raised the garage lid as silently as possible, but it squeaked and rattled, nonetheless. He flicked on a torch and directed its beam towards the back wall. Nicola's crumpled body was laying alongside the back wall. Her father had placed her brown leather jacket over her chest. Beneath it, her purple T-shirt was speckled with blood. The jacket might conceal blood stains but did nothing to keep her warm. *Not that she would have been bothered.* He tossed the jacket aside and dragged Nicola by her armpits out of the garage towards his van. He lifted her legs up between its open doors, clambered in, and dragged her along the floor.

In the distance, on the still air, he heard a police siren. He hastily bundled Nicola's body to one side, leapt out from the back of the van, slammed its back doors shut, raced around to the front, and dived into the driver's seat.

He turned the ignition key. The engine spluttered and faded. He needed petrol! He tried again. This time, the engine coughed into life and he prayed he had enough fuel to get him to the landfill otherwise he might well find himself eating his future meals from a prison cell.

※

John Payne approached the front door of his home. Marilyn was standing on the doorstep looking anxious. She was about to ask where the dickens had he been but took one look at the congealed blood on her husband's face and immediately phoned for an ambulance.

John protested but knew she was right. He might have a serious head injury. It had certainly hurt and when Marilyn touched one of the bruises he gasped and drew back in pain.

❄ ❄ ❄

Owen was well aware of the fact that Nigel had been stealing items of value from the supermarket. Now, as he sat in his in-law's home, given sick leave from work, he mulled over his options.

He had stolen items of very little value, and mainly for Owen, but Jason thought nothing of stealing electrical goods, LPs and even medicines from the dispensary. He could - *should* - report Jason to management but that would implicate *him*. At the very best, he would be sacked, and he needed his job, even though it was poorly paid.

Nicola wouldn't be able to return to her place of work at Greggs as she now had Owen to care for. Nursery fees were too high to afford. It would cost more in fees than Greggs paid her.

Of course, at this point, Owen did not know that Nicola would never be returning.

✻ ✻ ✻

"Have you contacted the police about your daughter?" the nurse asked.

"They can't bring her back, can they?" he replied miserably.

"No ... but they can catch whoever is responsible and prevent it happening to someone else."

"I'd like to catch that person *myself!*" John Payne retorted. "Give them back some of their own medicine ... *and then a bit!*"

"Whoever's responsible for this wickedness is targeting your family, don't you think?"

John fell silent for a moment and then looked up sharply.

"I really don't think I should be talking about this to you - no offence. You're right, though. Maybe my family could use some protection until such time as they catch the murdering swine! I'm sorry – excuse my language."

The nurse smiled. "No worries," she said and immediately recognised the foolishness of her remark.

"Can I go home now?" John asked. "My wife will walk me home."

At that moment, the door to the ward opened and a uniformed police officer started walking towards them.

"Do you feel up to making a statement, sir? Or if you're not up to it, perhaps you could call into the station when you're ready?"

"I'll talk to you now," John Payne replied. He looked up at the nurse.

"Is there somewhere more private we can go?" he asked.

"Of course. Follow me, please."

※ ※ ※

John Payne turned on the television in their living room and settled in beside Marilyn on the settee where they always watched the local evening news together. Tonight's programme promised to be distressing for them but nevertheless …

'Police are continuing their search for the missing body of Nicola Payne who was murdered on December 14th, 1991. Her body had been taken to a lock-up garage

adjoining a block of flats where it was discovered by her father, John Payne, who had himself been attacked and rendered unconscious. He later regained consciousness only to discover that he had been flung beside his daughter's lifeless corpse.

During his period of unconsciousness, however, the body of Nicola had been removed.

Anyone who was out on the night of December 14th and, in particular, on the Black Pad or **Woodway Close**, *and saw any unusual activity taking place is asked to contact the police as soon as they can.*

Miss Payne was 5ft 3in tall, of medium build, with brown hair and brown eyes. She was wearing a brown leather jacket, purple T-shirt and fawn trousers on the day of her disappearance.'

Marilyn turned to her husband.

"Nicola was with you in that filthy garage. Someone returned to it while you were unconscious and removed her body. Why would they do that?"

John Payne shrugged his shoulders and held his wife's hand tightly.

"Perhaps he thought he'd left his fingerprints on her clothing."

"Then his fingerprints would be on *your* clothing, too, surely?"

John frowned. "You're right, you know. The police missed a trick there."

"Well …" Marilyn began, "they would have to match

your prints to those of somebody already known to them, I suppose?"

John sighed. "I suppose so. Let's wait and see what tomorrow brings."

"I hope you don't mind but I promised Jason I'd look after Owen tomorrow. I thought he could do with a little time to himself. It's been such a terrible shock."

A tear fell from John's eye. "It's been a shock to us all," he said.

※ ※ ※

Nigel Barwell thought hard about any incriminating evidence that he might have left at the scenes of his crimes.

He cursed himself as he realised that he had forgotten to remove the two wooden tent pegs that had tripped up Nicola Payne and her father. He set out to retrieve them.

It was another cold, December morning when he parked his van close to the *Black Pad* once again and strolled along the track that had become so familiar to him. It was a short walk and he soon came across one of the wooden tent pegs. The rope was not attached to it. Over to his right, two young lads had hold of it and were swinging each other around in circles. This meant there would now be at least three sets of fingerprints on it. *That could prove useful*.

He called out to the boys and they turned towards him.

"What do you want, mister?" one called out.

"Have you come across another piece of wood like

this?" he asked, holding out one of the tent pegs he had found.

"It's a tent peg," the other lad said. "I know, 'cos I used some at Scout camp last summer."

"Yeah, I know, too" Nigel lied. "I'm a scout master. I was showing some of my lads how to erect a tent yesterday and accidentally left behind a couple of pegs, the tent bag ... and a piece of rope."

"Why did you need it ... the rope?"

"I was showing them how to tie knots."

The boys looked at each other and then the older of the two took a few steps to his right.

"You mean this?" he asked, holding up the length of frayed rope he had been messing around with.

"That's it!" Nigel exclaimed. "Give it here. Do you have the bag for them?"

"What d'you reckon?" the other boy asked his friend.

Before his friend had time to reply, a man out walking his dog approached them.

"Everything okay, lads? Is this man bothering you?"

"He says he wants this piece of rope."

"And these wooden tent pegs," the other added.

"And the bag they were in," the first lad said.

The dog began sniffing Nigel's trouser legs and he kicked it away.

"Hey, have a care!" the dog's owner shouted angrily. "That's my dog you're kicking!"

"He won't leave us alone," the younger boy insisted, pointing at Nigel and sensing an opportunity to stir up some trouble.

"Is that so? Well, I'll tell you what's going to happen." He turned to the older of the two boys.

"You're going to give me the rope and the pegs and the tatty bag they came in and I'm going to take them to the police station. You know why? Just before I set out this morning, I heard on the radio that they intend searching the *Black Pad* for a rope and two wooden pegs in connection with ... an incident."

He wasn't going to use the word *'murder'* in front of the young boys.

"So, please hand them over and *you* ..." and he now turned towards Nigel ... "tell me who you are and what your game is!"

Nigel regarded the man contemptuously. He was old and he had a walking stick. *No threat.*

"Damn you," he hissed and began jogging back down the track to his van.

❈ ❈ ❈

"This gentleman has just brought us some interesting objects that appear to have been discarded up on the *Black Pad.*"

The duty officer at Coventry Central Police Station was talking to an inspector from the Detective Division.

The detective studied the items that the dog-walker had

brought with him.

"Just for the record, could you tell me where you found these objects, please?"

"On the *Black Pad*. I was taking my dog for its daily walk and I saw two kids holding on to the ends of the rope and swinging each other around. They had a couple of tent pegs and a carrier bag on the ground beside them, too,"

"Did they mention where the rope had come from?"

"No ... simply that they'd come across it stretched across the track."

"Stretched between these?" and the policeman pointed at the two wooden pegs, dirty with dried mud.

"I guess so ... the lad said he'd almost tripped on the

rope."

"And how did you come by them ... just asking ... routine questions."

"The lads were being harassed by a man demanding they hand them over to him. Said he was a scout master ... if that's of any help."

The police officers looked thoughtful but said nothing until ...

"Truth be told... I watched the news last night on tv ... about Nicola Payne ... being found in a garage ... and then not being there ... if you follow. I wanted to take the credit for finding something that might prove helpful."

"Of course. Now, if you wouldn't mind following me through to an interview room, I'll ask for a description of the man you saw and go through your story again ... from the moment you left home right up to your arrival at our front desk."

※ ※ ※

Jason returned to work, stocking shelves overnight, at the supermarket. The staff were sympathetic and horrified at his loss. They hoped the police discovered the murderer's identity before somebody else suffered a similar fate.

During a late-night tea-break, he was approached by Nigel Barwell.

"Hey, Jason. Sorry to hear about Nicola. What a terrible thing to happen."

"Yeah, well ..."

"So, who's looking after your little boy?"

"Nicola's mum ... my mother-in-law."

"Full-time, I guess?"

"Pretty well, mate. I drop him off at her house on my way to work in the evening, finish my shift, come home for some sleep, collect him in the afternoon and take care of him during the day."

"Sounds like hard work."

"No kidding."

"Tell you what ..." Nigel began, "If you want a break some days, you could drop him off at my house and the missus would look after him for you. It'd give your mother-in-law a bit of a break."

Jason heard alarm bells ring in his head.

"No, you're okay, but I appreciate the offer."

"No probs. Any time, though. You've only to ask."

"Thanks, mate."

Jason worked hard that night and his line-manager told him he could head off twenty minutes sooner. He muttered his thanks and fetched his coat and gloves from the staff room. There was a staff entrance-and-exit door and he used it to walk out into the car park. As he passed by a scattering of staff cars, he spotted Nigel's mud-splattered van parked at an angle across two bays.

If I was lucky enough to have a car, he thought, I'd keep it looking a lot cleaner than that. There were a couple of floodlights overlooking the vehicles and the beam from one fell on the rear of Nigel's van.

Something caught Jason's eye and he knelt beside the bumper. The sill beneath the tailgate door was smeared with reddish … mud? Surely not? There hadn't been any rain for a week or so.

The smear had trickled down the rear bumper of the van and dried into a clot. He tried peering through the two panel windows of the door, but it was too dark to make out anything. If only he could take another look …*in daylight*. It was just a thought.

❈ ❈ ❈

Jason went to bed almost as soon he arrived back home from his shift at the supermarket. Later, when he went to his in-laws to collect Owen, he'd return to the track across the *Black Pad* and take a closer look at the route that Nicola would have taken on the day of her disappearance.

※

Nigel finished his shift a couple of minutes before Jason and stood outside the staff exit door. He didn't like what he saw. What he saw was Jason crouched at the rear of his van and looking closely at the bumper and then standing back up and peering through the panel windows. He doubted he would see much, if anything, in the darkness.

Nigel cursed. He should have put his van through the carwash at the far end of the car park but it had shut down by the time he'd turned up for his shift. He hung back and waited until Jason walked away before striding out towards his van. He turned the key in the ignition, revved the engine and drove away He was in for a shock.

As he approached the residents' garages by the block of flats, he spotted a police car parked to one side of the shingle forecourt and pulled up beside it. *I hope he doesn't check if I'm insured!*

"Have you caught the person who broke into my garage?" he asked the police officer.

"This is *your* garage, sir?"

"'Fraid so. Dreadful thing, eh? Do you know when I can have it back?"

"Forensics are still going over it. We've got your contact details, though. You've got one of those flats?" He pointed towards the apartment block.

"Yeah. Bit of a dump but beggars can't be choosers. Anyway, what are you looking for?"

"Just taking a look," the officer replied casually. "Back at the station, the sarge thought I might come across something that's been missed. You know ... a fresh set of eyes."

"Yeah, right. Well, have you found anything?"

"Two transistor radios still in their boxes with price tags attached and *'Morrisons'* printed along the top. A toaster and an electric iron. Do much ironing then?" the officer asked looking at Nigel's crumpled shirt and slacks. "Do you have a receipt for them?"

"They're not mine," Nigel said.

"I believe you, sir. Would you mind stepping across to my car, please?"

※ ※ ※

Jason set off along path through the *Black Pad*. He was tired but would catch up on an hour or two's sleep before collecting Owen from his grandparent's house.

December's air was still crisp but it was dry and firm underfoot as he followed the track. He didn't know quite what he expected to find but the police *might* have missed something. That was always a possibility.

He'd picked up a short tree branch close to the entrance to the *Black Pad* and used it to prod clumps of grass and poke amongst their blades. He nudged aside a cluster of dandelions that had grown steadily during the winter months and there, beneath their delicate heads, the thin, winter sun sparkled on something revealed by the branch.

Nicola had been *so* excited the day Jason had presented her with the beautiful silver necklace with her name attached at the centre of the chain ... and now, there it was, glinting amongst the dandelions and looking like a lost, forlorn memory.

"Do you have receipts for the items my constable has just placed on the counter?"

"I don't keep receipts. I don't know where they are. I've probably lost them."

"Can you explain why there are security tags attached to the items and how they came to be in your garage?"

"The girl at the checkout probably forgot to remove the tags."

The two police officers smiled at each other.

"Correct me if I'm wrong, Mister Barwell ... I don't work in a supermarket, unfortunately. I'm stuck behind this desk dealing with criminals ... but doesn't an alarm sound if someone tries to nick an item with a security tag attached?"

"I guess," Nigel replied.

"You *guess*?"

"Someone must have put them there. That guy that got himself locked in, maybe."

"Or was *locked* in, perhaps? He could hardly lock

himself in from inside, sir. Just stay where you are for a minute, will you?"

Nigel considered making a break for the entrance door but that's not something an innocent person would do.

So, he remained where he was.

He didn't have to wait long.

"This way, please, Mister Barwell. I'm DS Prescott. I'm heading up the team dealing with the murder of Nicola Payne and the attempted murder of her father. I need you to answer a few questions. It shouldn't take long. You'll be on your way in no time."

※ ※ ※

"You last took your van from the garage was when …

the night before the body was first discovered?"

"I took it towards the *Black Pad*. I like to drive out there some nights and look at the moon and the stars. I find it relaxing."

"And did you *see* the moon and lots of stars after what, I believe, had been an unusually foggy day?"

"Yeah. You've got to wonder, though, haven't you? I mean … how they stay up there?"

"Er … forces of gravity, no doubt. *I* have to wonder how you managed to see them, though, what with dense fog hanging over the *Black Pad* that day and into the night."

Nigel shifted uneasily on the uncomfortable wooden chair.

"Maybe the fog had cleared while I was there."

"Maybe. Anyway, let's move on from there, shall we? Having had your fill of the heavens, you then returned to your flat?"

"Yeah, that's right."

"Was that before or after you drove your van into the garage?"

"Er … *after* I think."

"*Think* for a moment. Which was it? Before or after?"

"I remember now. I unlocked the garage and drove straight in. There were no bodies in there - just the gear you found at the back."

"Which you had stolen from the supermarket where you work?"

"Yeah, that's right." A charge of theft was preferable to one of murder.

"And *then* you returned to your flat?"

"Yeah."

The police detective stared at Nigel.

"Are you sure of that?" He noted Nigel's hesitation and added,

"It's just that we have a witness who lives opposite the *Black Pad* who swears he saw your van return there early evening."

"He got that wrong, then. It would've been too foggy for him to have seen my van."

"*But not too foggy for you to see the stars?*"

The detective continued.

"And then he swears you returned ten minutes later dragging a flat, wooden trolley with something bulky on it."

"He's mistaken."

"From a distance of twenty yards?"

"He'd have needed glasses to see that far!"

"He *was* wearing glasses."

"Did you steal the trolley from the supermarket?"

"Of course not. It's mine."

"With the supermarket's name on the handle?"

Nigel's face reddened.

"Okay - yes, I *did* borrow it."

"Thank you. For what purpose?"

Nigel thought fast.

"It was my workmate, Jason. He wanted me to keep an eye out for his wife, Nicola. Said she should have been at his mother-in-law's but hadn't turned up. Jason said she'd planned to go across the *Black Pad*. I drove there to take a look. To help out a friend from work."

"Why did you need a trolley?"

"Reckoned she might have tripped and twisted her

ankle and been unable to walk. No way I could carry her very far ... so I drove straight to the supermarket and put a trolley in the back of my van."

"And then you went to look for her?"

"That's right."

The detective pointed to a hump-shaped mound on his desk and removed a cloth that covered it.

"Do you recognise these items?" he asked.

Nigel gasped.

"Do I take that to be a '*yes?*'"

He had forgotten to remove the pegs and the rope from the Black Pad! There was the bag, too. Stupid! Stupid! He should have picked them up and loaded them on the cart along with Nicola's body before those two kids had found them. The kids had handed them to the old guy with a stick and the old guy with the stick must have taken them to the police station.

"I've never seen those before in my life," he said.

"You know what they are, though?"

"'Course I do!"

"Tell me."

Nigel was wary. "A bit of old rope and some sticks."

"What do you think the *sticks* might be used for?"

"I've no idea."

"You've never been camping then?"

"No," Nigel replied. "I like my comfort too much. I

prefer to sleep on a mattress. Can I go now?"

The police detective smiled.

"'Course you can but I'll have a couple of my chaps accompany you ... just to see you come to no harm."

"What sort of harm?"

"Well, there's a murderer on the loose. You wouldn't want to confront him on your own now, would you?"

"I'll be okay," Nigel muttered.

The officer grinned.

"Maybe I should have mentioned this sooner ... we have a court order authorising us to conduct a search of your flat."

Nigel's eyes opened wide. He caught his breath and gasped.

※

Jason stared at the silver necklace and tears filled his eyes. So, was this the spot where Nicola was murdered? A well-used, well-worn track across a bleak tract of grassland known to locals as the *Black Pad*?

The police had conducted a search of the route Nicola was most likely to have taken to reach her parent's house. The papers reported the discovery of two tent pegs, a length of rope and a bag. There was no mention of the necklace that nestled in the warm pocket of Jason's winter coat.

※

Nigel just wanted to get in his van and drive as far away as he could ... instead of which he was sitting next to a police officer on the rear seat of a police car and being driven from the police station to his flat on **Copperas Street, Aldermans Green, Coventry. His mind raced.** *He knew what they would find.*

※

Nigel's flat was a modest affair. To reach it, one had to climb two flights of stairs - either that or make use of the grubby lift - if it was working. Nigel pushed open the entrance door to the building and headed towards the lift. The police officers followed closely behind.

Taped beside the lift's metal framework, a sign read:

'Lift out of order. Please use the stairs.'

It was frequently out of action.

They ascended the spiral staircase.

Nigel asked himself whether he should say he'd mislaid the key to his flat's door but they might then use physical force to smash their way in ... so he unlocked it and they all went in.

The policemen were uncomfortably thorough and worked quickly. They left Nigel's bedroom to last.

One officer searched the contents of a bedside cabinet whilst the other headed to a wardrobe.

Nigel knew what the man would find.

"Over here, Jim! Look what I've just found!"

※

Less than an hour later, Nigel found himself facing DC Prescott once more. He had sat in the same police car, with the same two officers and been taken back to the same police station,

"Do you do much camping?" DS Prescott asked.

"What? In the middle of winter? What do *you* think?"

"I'm more interested in knowing what *you* think, Nigel."

"I think I'd be crazy to go camping in December."

"*Are* you crazy?"

"What sort of a question is that? You can't speak to me like that. I have my rights."

"And some of us have our *wrongs*, Nigel. Tell me ...

just for the record ... when did you last make use of your tent?"

"I don't know ... oh, yeah ... in July. I went to a folk festival and there was an area set aside for campers."

"Can you recall how you secured the tent?"

"*Uh?*"

"How did you fix it to the ground?" D C Prescott asked in a patient tone.

"With pegs, of course!"

Prescott spoke into his intercom.

"Would you bring that stuff through to me, Jim?"

A few moments later the door opened and an officer entered carrying a tent bag.

He looked questioningly at his boss.

"It's okay. Just put it on my desk."

Prescott opened the bag and withdrew a wooden peg.

"Recognise this?" he asked.

"I dunno. It's a bit of wood. Might be a tent peg."

"As an experienced camper, you know darned well that it's a tent peg."

"So what?"

"Two of these were found on the *Black Pad*. Did you forget to take them home with you?"

"They're not mine."

"*Really?* Admittedly, they don't have your name

written on them, but they would appear to be a good match for the others that we found in your flat."

"They all look the same. Could be anyone's."

"We'll see."

The detective returned to the bag and withdrew a length of rope.

"We discovered this, too, attached to a second tent peg."

"So?"

"So where did you get this?"

"I didn't get it from anywhere. It's nothing to do with me."

"But wouldn't you attach guy ropes to the wooden

pegs?"

"Maybe."

"Mister Barwell ... did you erect a tent on the *Black Pad* on or before the night of December 14th, 1991?"

Nigel Barwell answered the question truthfully.

"I did not."

"We found tracks along the path that match those of your cart."

Nigel was about to respond but the detective held up his hand.

"We also discovered footprints that we believe are yours."

"You can't know that. Lots of people go out along that track."

"But maybe not mid-winter in dense fog."

Nigel shrugged his shoulders again.

"In the same spot that we discovered what we believe to be your footprints we also found those of Nicola Payne and …" he raised his hand as Nigel opened his mouth to speak, "… and the tracks made by what we believe to be your cart. A tent bag was brought to our attention, too."

"And that's it? Nothing more than guesswork?"

"Not quite, Nigel. You see, the neighbour, who swears he spotted your van make two journeys towards the *Black Pad,* had the presence of mind to take a snapshot on the second occasion. Admittedly, it's a poor photo, what with the fog and all but, when blown up, the make and registration is clearly visible. And you know what … surprise, surprise … it's matches *your* vehicle. "

"I never said I wasn't there, did I?"

"But you can see how suspicious it looks, can't you?"

"I've not done anything."

"And yet we also have in our possession a tent bag containing more pegs, more rope and a rubber mallet."

"So?"

"So, Mister Barwell, *did you kill Nicola Payne* … and if so, *why?*"

"*No!* Why aren't you questioning Jason. He was

nicking stuff from the supermarket, too, you know."

"Really? Next thing, you'll be telling me his baby son's a stalker!"

In a softer tone, DS Prescott added,

"Anyway, I think that's enough chat for one day. You may leave now but don't travel outside of Coventry. If further evidence comes to light that links you to Nicola Payne's disappearance, I'd like to know where I can find you."

※

Jason dropped Owen off at his mother-in-law's house and set off walking to work. As he approached the staff entrance, a voice called out to him.

"Hey, Jason! Hold up a minute."

Jason could have done without this.

"Not going in then?" he asked disinterestedly.

"Someone snitched on me. I've been sacked."

"Well, don't look at me, mate. What you get up to is your business. Anyway, sorry to hear it. Are they reporting it to the police?"

"The police? No, thanks all the same. They're trying to collar me for your girlfriend's disappearance."

"Nicola? Why? How are you involved?"

"I'm not but ..."

"Jason! Are you coming in to work today or what?"

It was Jason's line manager.

"Sorry, mate. Have to go or I'll be sacked, too."

The supermarket might have fired Nigel for his thieving but, to his credit, Nigel hadn't snitched on him.

※ ※ ※

Each day that passed, without being arrested, boosted Nigel's confidence. Almost every day that passed, he was tempted to drive to the landfill to do ... *what*? Something daft ... to see if a hand or a foot was protruding from the mountains of trash?

He'd told the guy at the refuse centre that he was getting rid of an old, rolled up carpet. A most unusual carpet, too, as it had pieces of rag stuffed into both open ends and pieces of strong rope at close intervals along its length.

He had experienced a moment of panic as he flung the

bundle down into the waste pit. *As it landed, the impact dislodged a knot, a gap appeared and a hand emerged.*

❋❋❋

He could never feel certain that his activities were not being observed. Not that there was ever much for anyone to see. He didn't go out much, didn't have a job, didn't have much spare cash left over from his unemployment handout. He had plenty of spare time, though. Plenty of spare time to worry whether or not the police would catch up with him.

❋❋❋

New advancements in forensics resulted in Nicola's DNA being found on the jacket that she had been wearing at the time and which had been recovered in 1991 from the garage where her body had been dumped. It didn't explain how her DNA got there, though, and the police were no closer to discovering her murderer.

It was to take a further five years, until April of 1996, to be precise, that Detective Prescott, now an Inspector, received a tip-off from an anonymous source. He quickly put together a team of men to excavate the garden of a property in Woodway Lane. His team spent twelve hours searching for Nicola's remains but nothing was found. It was eventually dismissed as one neighbour being vindictive towards another.

The newspapers continued to speculate on the killer's identity, however, and the whereabouts of Nicola's body, but the leads led only to dead ends. *So to speak.*

Jason often wondered if Nigel had been responsible for Nicola's death and, in the darker moments, whether he had intended targeting other members of his family, namely young Owen or his in-laws, Marilyn and John Payne. He was convinced that John Payne had suffered at the hands of Nigel but the police could find nothing to connect Nigel to the attack.

Nicola's parents never gave up in their attempts to find their daughter's murderer and they initiated numerous appeals, each urging the public to help find her.

However, the years passed and the police failed to find answers to their inquiries before the tragic death of her mother, aged seventy-seven.

In 2012, an article appeared in the local newspaper. It had been written by David Williams, a family friend, the man who had taken the photograph of Nigel

Barwell's van on the day of Nicola's disappearance. David was seventy-six when he wrote:

'I remember the night that it happened well. It was ever so misty. You could not see a thing. It was real thick fog so nobody would have seen anything untoward.

She went walking across the path and never made it. Half an hour later her dad went out looking for her and phoned the police.

The family have never given up looking for her but they do think she is dead. It is the biggest mystery in Coventry. It has never gone away.

I never believed what Nigel Barwell told police - someone broke into his garage and somehow started the engine and taken his van which he later found on the edge of the Black Pad.'

※

For three decades, detectives, together with assistance from private investigators, had conducted numerous searches of properties, gardens, rivers, a canal, a lake and woodland. Despite one of the largest search operations in British history, involving helicopters, dogs, divers, and more than 100 officers, no trace of Nicola's body had ever been found.

※

The years passed and Owen, the baby, grew into Owen, the man. He had turned thirty-one and had never given up hope of discovering who it was that had taken his mother from him.

Then there came a day when he and his father, Jason,

drove to the local landfill site with a wobbly table that needed disposing of. They were uncertain to which area it needed taking and approached a site employee.

"*Jason*!" the man exclaimed.

"Sorry ... should I know you?" Jason asked.

"You won't remember me, but we were at school together. I read about your poor wife in the paper. I'm really sorry,"

Jason shrugged his shoulders.

"That was a long while ago. Life goes on."

"But I bet your mate's old van didn't go on for long."

"Sorry? What do you mean?"

"Years ago, he turned up here in a dirty old van and

walked across the yard with a bundle wrapped around his shoulders ... seemed unsure where to dump it. I asked what he had, and he said he had an old carpet to dispose of. He was doing his mate, Jason, a favour because Jason didn't have his own transport."

Jason felt faint. "How long ago was that?" he asked.

"Now you're asking ... at least thirty years, I reckon. I was a handsome young man back then ... now look at me! I'm retiring next year while I still have my faculties!"

"Can you describe the man?"

"There you go again! Just as well I've still got a brain in my head."

Jason listened carefully as the man began ...

"I thought he looked a bit scruffy but it was his van that really caught my attention. It was filthy ... covered in mud and the windows were so dirty I'm surprised he could see out of them. Couldn't have been legal."

"Was he about my height?" Jason asked.

"An inch or two shorter, maybe. Scruffily dressed. I pointed him towards '*BULKY ITEMS*'. He dumped the carpet in the container and drove off with smoke pouring from the van's exhaust."

"Where do those containers go? When they leave here?"

"There's a landfill site a few miles from here. I don't think you'll get the old carpet back, though! Anyway, let's get rid of that table of yours."

*

Nigel Barwell! Without a doubt, Nigel Barwell had taken a journey to the rubbish tip many, many years ago and that is where he had dumped Nicola's body.

If only he could lay his hands on that piece of filth ... Well, if *he* couldn't, he knew who *could*!

*

"*Nicola Payne?* You're joking?"

Jason drew in his breath. "I don't consider the abduction and murder of my wife to be a joke! Now, who's in charge here?"

The desk sergeant's face reddened and he mumbled an apology. "

"It's Detective Chief Inspector Martin Slevin that you

need to speak to. I'll check if he's in his office ... and I apologise for being such an idiot."

Jason remained silent, waited, and a few minutes later the desk sergeant reappeared.

"Would you follow me, Mister Payne. The DCI is keen to speak with you."

※

Jason recounted his experience at the refuse depot and the DCI listened carefully to what he was being told.

When Jason had completed his tale, the DCI asked him to go through it a second time. He wanted to confirm that the details were the same on a retelling.

"Do you mind if I take some notes this time?" he asked

politely.

※

The police visited the homes of two men and arrested them both. One was Nigel Barwell and the other

Thomas O'Reilly. Each was charged with the murder of Nicola Payne and both protested their innocence and denied any involvement in the disappearance of Nicola Payne.

Even after thirty years, the yard employee from the refuse site picked out Nigel Barwell at an identity parade. At first, Barwell had refused to take part but he changed his mind when it was pointed out to him that his refusal might be used against him in evidence by prosecutors.

With the advances in forensic science that had taken place, the cold-case investigation team now found it possible to make a crucial discovery. Jason had shown them the necklace that he'd found on the *Black Pad* thirty years earlier. He had kept it safe even though it brought only sadness and tears to his eyes each time he read the name *'Nicola'*. By making use of Deoxyribonucleic acid (DNA), forensics had been able to match the fingerprints on the necklace to those found on the wooden tent pegs and rope obtained thirty years earlier by DS Prescott. *They were the fingerprints of Nigel Barwell.*

※ ※ ※

"The prosecution alleges that Nigel Barwell and

Thomas O'Reilly acted together to murder 18-year-old Nicola Payne, a mother of one, and then disposed of her body, which has never been found."

Under cross-examination from prosecutor Andrew Smith QC at Birmingham Crown Court, Mr Barwell insisted he had never met Nicola Payne, or her brother, Scott, and rejected claims he had been attracted to Miss Payne when he had once seen her in a pub with Jason.

※※※

"I would like to call my first witness," Andrew Smith QC, the prosecutor, announced to the court.

"Woud you tell the court your name and where you live please?"

"Patrick Carter, Woodway Walk, Coventry."

"Could you tell the court what it was you saw on December 14, 1991?"

"I left my house at about 12.15pm on December 14, 1991, to take my dog on its daily walk. I took my usual route along Winston Avenue, Coventry to the Black Pad.

I noticed two men standing beside a blue Ford Capri which was parked behind the power station on the edge of land known locally as 'the Black Pad'" the Nicola Payne murder trial heard.

"A short time later, I heard a woman scream."

Reading from a previous statement to police while giving evidence the previous Friday (October 16), Mr Carter said,

"I saw a man standing in bushes by a tree about five yards away from me. When the person saw me they moved behind the tree."

Patrick Carter then added,

"I could not tell if it was a man or woman. The person might have been nearly 6ft tall and was wearing a brown leather jacket. I could hear a revving noise coming from a car which appeared to be coming from behind the bush."

The court heard that when he went around the bush onto the road he saw a metallic blue Ford Capri.

Mr Carter said *"a man stood next to the back corner of the car, parked in the lane leading away from the recreation ground"*.

He added: *"I believe it was a second man to the one I*

saw the first time."

He described him as white, about 6ft 3ins with hair parted on the right-hand side and wearing a brown leather jacket and pale blue jeans.

Mr Carter said he "*heard the man summon his dog and kneel down beside it, while he continued to walk past the car which bore a registration plate around 1980.*"

The court heard that the car had larger than standard wheels which appeared to be chrome although they were quite dirty. It had a back spoiler which looked '*a bit tacky*', and it had a chrome exhaust.

"*When I had walked past the car a few feet I heard a female scream. It lasted a short period of time, not very long,*" he said.

"*It wasn't excessively loud and seemed to be muffled*

and came from the direction of the bushes I had just walked past."

He continued, *"by the time I looked back the person had gone but the car was still there."*

Mr Carter said he stopped and waited, looking at the bushes for four or five minutes before he began to head towards the fields and Potters Green Road.

"I went back to see if the car was still there to get the registration number," he added, *"but when I got back to the lane where the Capri was it had gone."*

Mr Carter said "*I got back home around 12.45pm and did not hear about a missing person until the Sunday afternoon. I made a statement to the police about 7pm that day.*"

He added that when he arrived at the police station in

Coventry he noticed a pale blue metallic Ford Capri in the car park.

"It was very similar in colour to the Capri I had seen on the previous day," Mr Carter said.

Nigel Barwell, aged 51, from Copperas Street, and Thomas O'Reilly, 51, of Ribble Road, both Coventry, deny murdering Nicola, who went missing on the same day, December 14, 1991. The trial continues ...

※

Nigel Barwell tells the court:

"I had never laid eyes on Nicola Payne, it's as simple as that."

The prosecution put it to Mr Barwell that he had spoken

to Scott Payne, who gave evidence last month, at a pub in 1991.

Mr Barwell replied that it did not happen.

"Whilst we feel very sorry for the Payne family and we understand the grief and the heartache they are going through, Scott Payne came to court and he lied to the court."

Brothers-in-law Nigel Barwell and Thomas O'Reilly denied the charges against them and are cleared by a jury of killing Nicola Payne.

Nigel Barwell's life was a total mess. He was unable to hold down a job. He was short of money. He never had enough to buy the drugs that he'd become addicted to

... so he found a solution that solved both problems. He bought and sold them. He made money as a drug dealer.

However, it was not long before he again made the local newspaper's headlines.

'A Coventry man who threatened to get a gun and kill a police officer and then turn the weapon on himself will be sentenced today, 21 March 2017.'

Nigel Barwell's shocking statement came after a stressful few years which included standing trial accused of killing missing mum Nicola Payne.'

His barrister said that Nigel *'had spent a total of two years on remand before and during the high-profile trial and this added to already existing mental health problems and resulted in the outburst.'*

Barwell, 52, of Copperas Street, Bell Green, pleaded guilty to the offence which happened last May while attending an appointment at Cofa Court, in Coventry, to assess his capability for employment and benefits.'

Henry Skudra, for the prosecution, told the court that Barwell, a dad-to-five, *'was telling the nurse about his troubles with mental health problems and post-traumatic stress disorder (PTSD).'*

Mr Skudra explained that it was at this point that Barwell had said, *'I'm going to get a gun and shoot police and then myself and it will happen.'*

Shudra continued, "*that led the nurse to believe he was*

telling the truth and also due to the calm and collected manner in which it was said."

After the appointment, *'the nurse rang police and Barwell was subsequently arrested."*

Police interviewed Barwell about his comment but he replied, "*no comment."*

Fergus Malone was Nigel Barwell's representative and he explained how his client "*has had a number of 'life events' over the past few years and these included being charged with the murder of missing Coventry mum Nicola Payne who left her boyfriend's house in December 1991 and was never seen again."*

Following a six-week trial, Malone added, "*Barwell,*

alongside his brother-in-law Thomas O'Reilly, were found not guilty following a six-week trial in 2015'.

Furthermore, Fergus Malone explained,
"He was on remand for fourteen months before the trial and then on remand in prison for a further ten months. His was a high-profile case with a lot of press attention. He struggled with the prison environment", and then pointed out that Barwell *"had been out of trouble since 2003. He is not proud of his record of old but the real offending on that goes back a long time."*

Referring to the threat 'to get a gun and kill a police officer' Malone pointed out that when Barnwell made the threats *"he was under a lot of stress as he was being probed about some of his experiences which he found stressful."*

Continuing, he said that *'although a criminal comment, it had no substance to it. It could be seen as a cry for help,"* pointing out that *'when police searched Barwell's home following the threats, no gun or other weapon was found.'*

The court then heard a psychologist state that *'it is not uncommon for people coming out of a long time on remand to struggle to re-adapt to civilian life.'*
Judge de Bertodano passed sentence and then told Barwell: *'Please, please be careful what you say. Whatever you are feeling, other people can get scared by what you say. This has put you back here where you don't want to be. At the age of 52, I hope that this is the last time I see you in this court."*

Jason felt weary. He hadn't slept well. Maybe age is catching up with me, he thought ... or maybe I have too many things on my mind.

He took the short walk to a newsagent and bought a copy of the local newspaper and then covered another hundred steps to the mini-market where he bought a *baton* for his breakfast.

He hadn't remarried. Nobody could replace Nicola. Time passes, he thought, but not so its memories.

※

Jason sat at his dining room table with his *baton* sliced down its centre and filled with margarine and slices of mature cheddar. He liked to browse his local newspaper while he ate.

He opened *The Coventry Observer*. It was dated 21st of August 2024 and his eyes travelled down the front page until it reached the headline to a fresh article by *The Observer* crime reporter.

'Police are investigating the 'unexplained' death of a man in Coventry.'

'Officers were called to Roseberry Avenue in Bell Green on Tuesday, January 30, 2024.

Paramedics were also called to Roseberry Avenue at around 10.15am on Tuesday. Crews found a man at the scene, said West Midlands Ambulance Service.

Medics said nothing could be done to save the man and he was sadly pronounced dead. Detectives say they are working to identify the man and are currently treating his death as 'unexplained.'

Nicola's brother, Scott, had previously offered a reward of £10,000 for information leading to the recovery of Nicola's body. He now tripled the amount to £30,000.

Nigel Barwell had always denied ever going to the refuse site. There was no evidence to disprove his assertion. His van had been scrapped many years earlier and the site employee could not be certain that the appearance of the far older Barwell resembled that of 1991.

Neither Nicola Payne's body nor her remains have ever been found.

Drug dealer Nigel Barwell

Nicola Payne went missing in broad daylight on December 14, 1991, in Wood End, Coventry, while walking across land known locally as the Black Pad, to her parents' home.

Nicola Payne disappeared from Coventry in December 1991

The disappearance of Nicola Payne on December 14th, 1991.

TIMELINE OF THE STORY SO FAR:

It has been more than 30 years since young mum Nicola Payne was last seen and her disappearance remains one of the biggest unsolved cases in the UK. It's a case that has Coventry at its core and is one that has hung over the city for more than three decades and the hunt for the truth remains unanswered.

April 1996: Police excavate the garden of a property in Woodway Lane, acting on a tip-off, but after 12 hours of searching nothing is found.

Summer 2001: Part of the Oxford Canal, in Ansty, is dredged after a witness comes forward with fresh information, but nothing is found.

September 2001: Bones are found near to where Nicola disappeared but turn out to be animal remains.

2005: A new poster campaign is launched round the country to bring the case back into the public eye.

2006: Nicola's picture appears on t-shirts printed by the National Missing Persons Helpline.

March 2007: It is announced that the case is to be re-examined. The Major Investigation Unit based at Chace Avenue police station takes on the investigation after potential lines of inquiry are identified. Parents John and Marilyn re-appeal for those with information to come forward. A statement is also read on behalf of Nicola's son Owen, by this time 16.

November 1, 2007: Police arrest a 37-year old man from Derbyshire on suspicion of the abduction and murder of Nicola. He is brought back to Chace Avenue police station for questioning and is released on bail pending further inquiries.

March 2008: The 37-year-old man is released from bail. No further action is taken against him.

June 11, 2008: Excavations begin at the garden of a house in Winston Avenue, Henley Green.

June 12, 2008: Searches at the house draw a blank.

June 19, 2012: After a tip-off police begin excavating land in Courthouse Green.

June 20, 2012: Two men, aged 74 and 45, are both arrested as part of the investigation. A back garden in Miles Meadow, Bell Green, is searched.

June 21, 2012: The 74-year-old is released without charge.

The 45-year-old is released on bail but charges against him are dropped in August.

December 14, 2012: Police and Nicola's parents launch the 21st anniversary appeal, asking for help identifying two men seen close to the Black Pad on the day she disappeared.

December 12, 2013: A forensic breakthrough in the case is announced.

December 2013: Two men, both aged 49, are arrestein the Aldermans Green and Stoke areas of the city on suspicion of Nicola's abduction and murder. A 51-year-old woman is also arrested in Aldermans Green on suspicion of perverting the course of justice.

January 2014: The two men and the woman are bailed.

February 2014: Police search grassland at Stoke Floods, near Mayflower Drive, Stoke Hill.

February 2014: A 49-year-old man and 47-year-old woman are arrested in connection with the disappearance. They are bailed until April.

March 2014: Police launch a search of Coombe Abbey Woodland.

January 2015: Nigel Barwell, aged 51, of Copperas Street, Aldermans Green, and Thomas O'Reilly, aged 50, of Ribble Road, Stoke, are charged with the murder of Nicola Payne.

April 2015: Barwell and O'Reilly plead not guilty to Nicola Payne's murder.

April 2015: Specialist police search Coombe Park Fishery.

June 2015: Underwater search held at Coombe Park Fisheries close to Coombe Abbey Country Park.

October 2015: Nicola Payne's murder trial starts.

November 2015: Brothers-in-law Nigel Barwell and Thomas O'Reilly are cleared by a jury of killing Nicola Payne.

November 2015: Following the trial, West Midlands Police say the case will remain open.

November 2016: Police resume the search for the body of Nicola Payne at Coombe Country Park.

December 2016: Nicola's family release new images of her on the anniversary of her disappearance.

December 2016: Nicola's brothers speak publicly for first time 25 years on.

January 2017: Searches continue in woodland at Coombe Country Park.

April 2017: Detective Chief Inspector Martin Slevin issues a clear message for those responsible: "Don't take the secret to your grave."

December 2017: On the 26th anniversary of her disappearance, Nicola's brother Scott announces a reward for information leading to Nicola being found had been tripled to £30,000.

March 2018: Divers search the fishing lake at Coombe Country Park. High-tech equipment is used in an attempt to find any human remains that may be at the beauty spot.

February 2020: Specialist divers begin a search of the Oxford Canal just outside Harborough Magna.

March 2020: Divers return to the canal in Ansty, Coventry to search around more bridges to look for a body.

March 2023: Nicola Payne's mum Marilyn dies without ever finding her.

129

Google: Amazon/books/Terence Braverman

amazon/books/terence braverman updates:

www.noteablemusic.co.uk

terry@terrybraverman.co.uk

* * *

AVAILABLE BOOKS (August 2024)

'Whiskers, Wings and Bushy Tails"

(Stories from The Undermead Woods) book series for children.

Large print and double line spacing

The Inner Mystic Circle

The Race

Curly Cat

Dotty Dormouse

Blackberry Pie

George and the Magic Jigsaw

Rain! Rain! Rain!

Where is Dotty Dormouse?

Tap! Tap! Tap!

SwaggerWagger

Three Wheels and a Bell

The Chase

Blackberry Bluff

Rebellion

Autumn

Quiz Night

Black as Night

Sheepish Singing Sisters

Ollie Owl's Experiment (Part Two)

Good Deeds and Evil Intentions

The New Age of Barter

The Mouse That Scored

Links of Gold

Buttercups and Daisies

The Tick-Tock 'Tective Agency and the Case of The Missing Tiddles

The Mysterious Case of the Missing Scarecrow

Carrots

Woof! Woof!

*****

Millie Manx (The Tale of a Tail)

Granddad Remembers (But is he telling the truth?)

Ninky and Nurdle (Stories from Noodle-Land)

The Playground of Dreams

What Can I Do When It's Raining Outside?

Buggy Babes

More...

CRIME

Time to Kill

Stage Fright

The Potato Eaters / Revolving Doors (Fiction based on fact)

Donald Dangle is on The Point of Murder

ROMANCE

The Man from Blue Anchor

The Night of The Great Storm

A TWIST IN THE TALE

(Open Pandora's Box and what will you find?) 25 stories with 'a twist in the tale':

A Night at the Castle

Baby Jane

The Little Bedroom

Bulls Eye

A Problem at School

A Running Joke

The Cure

Old Rocker

The New Appointment

The Sunflower

The Christmas Fairy

Pressure

Promotion

Knock, Knock, Knock

The Letter

Printed in Great Britain
by Amazon